Timothy Cox will NOT change his Socks

by ROBERT KINERK

Pictures by
STEPHEN GAMMELL

A Paula Wiseman Book
Simon & Schuster Books for Young Readers
New York   London   Toronto   Sydney

"What would happen, I wonder," said Timothy Cox,
"if I went a whole month without changing my socks?"
"I imagine," his dog said—a dachshund named Walt—
"that sooner or later some folks would find fault."
"True," Timmy said. "There are some I'd offend.
That shouldn't deter me, though, should it, old friend?
For you know very well, Walter, I'm the type who
gets an idea and then *follows it through*!"

Tim dressed the next morning and slicked down his hair.
Then he put on his socks—the very same pair
he'd removed from his feet just the evening before!
"Day one," he told Walt as he walked out his door.

His mother and father watched Timmy walk off.
They quietly said, "Though there's some who may scoff,
our boy, we believe, is the best ever seen.
He's courteous, beautiful, brilliant, and clean."

Tim rushed to his classroom and sat in his seat.
Did anyone notice the smell from his feet?
A few of his neighbors cast glances around.
Miss Claypoole, his teacher, stopped speaking and frowned.
That was it—nothing more. There was no one who yelled,
"What is that *stink*? It's the worst thing I've smelled!"

Timmy's socks the next morning smelled slightly like glue.
To his dachshund, when leaving, Tim said, "It's day two,
and nobody's said that they smell something strange."
Said the dog with a frown, "Well, I'm sure *that* will change."

That day Timmy sat with his hands on his desk,
knowing the smell was a bit more grotesque.
All the windows around him flew up before noon.
Miss Claypoole taught on, but she looked like she'd swoon.
Pupils wrinkled their noses, and just at the bell
a few of them asked, "What on earth is that smell?"

A registered letter came early next day.
It was brief. It was blunt. And it had this to say:
"Timothy, Timothy, Timothy Cox,
won't you consider, please, changing your socks?
Your friends and your neighbors are getting fed up!"
"And it's only day three," Timmy said to his pup.

That night Timmy lay with his eyes bright as lamps.
Next day his whole class, on their noses, wore clamps.
Into the classroom strode Principal Plum
with his nostrils squeezed shut by his finger and thumb.
He let Timmy know in hygienical prose
that his socks were an insult to everyone's nose.
"In conclusion, my boy," he harrumphed, "I must say
if you don't change your socks, then you must stay away."
He gave Timmy books and a long reading list
so when he came back there'd be nothing he'd missed.

Day four—and word spread. It had traveled for blocks.
"There is someone around here who won't change his socks!"
To the door of Tim's house came a neighbor, Miss Spear.
To Timothy's parents, she whispered, "I fear
someone you love may have not changed his socks.
Have you checked on your dear little Tim, Mrs. Cox?"

Tim's mother just laughed, and his dad said, "It's clear
you don't know our Timmy like we do, Miss Spear.
Our son's the most perfect young man we have seen—
athletic and witty, good-natured and clean."

Timothy, Timothy, Timothy Cox,
won't you consider, please, changing your socks?
That was written on signs that the neighbors put up.
"And it's only day six," Timmy said to his pup.

HELP!

TRY SOME SOAP

CHANGE YOUR SOCKS, PLEASE

The Board of Health officers called Timmy's father.
They told him, "Your son is becoming a bother.
He's healthy. He's hearty. He's strong as an ox.
And he ought to be *ordered* to change his darn socks!"

Tim's father replied in his courteous way,
"If you really knew Timmy, that's *not* what you'd say.
Let me send you a photo that shows what I mean.
My Timmy's genteel, artistic, and clean."

That night in his bed, with his blankets pulled high,
Tim said to his dachshund, "Two weeks have gone by!"
"Yes," said the dog, "and those socks that you're wearing
smell worse than a box full of overripe herring.
By now you should know, or at least I should think,
what happens to boys who wear stockings that stink.
And I'd like to suggest—as your pet, as your *friend*—
that it's time for this effort you're making to end."

"A month is a month," Timmy said to his dog.
With that he rolled over and slept like a log,
while Walter gazed up at the sky, which was vast,
and prayed that the month would go by very fast.

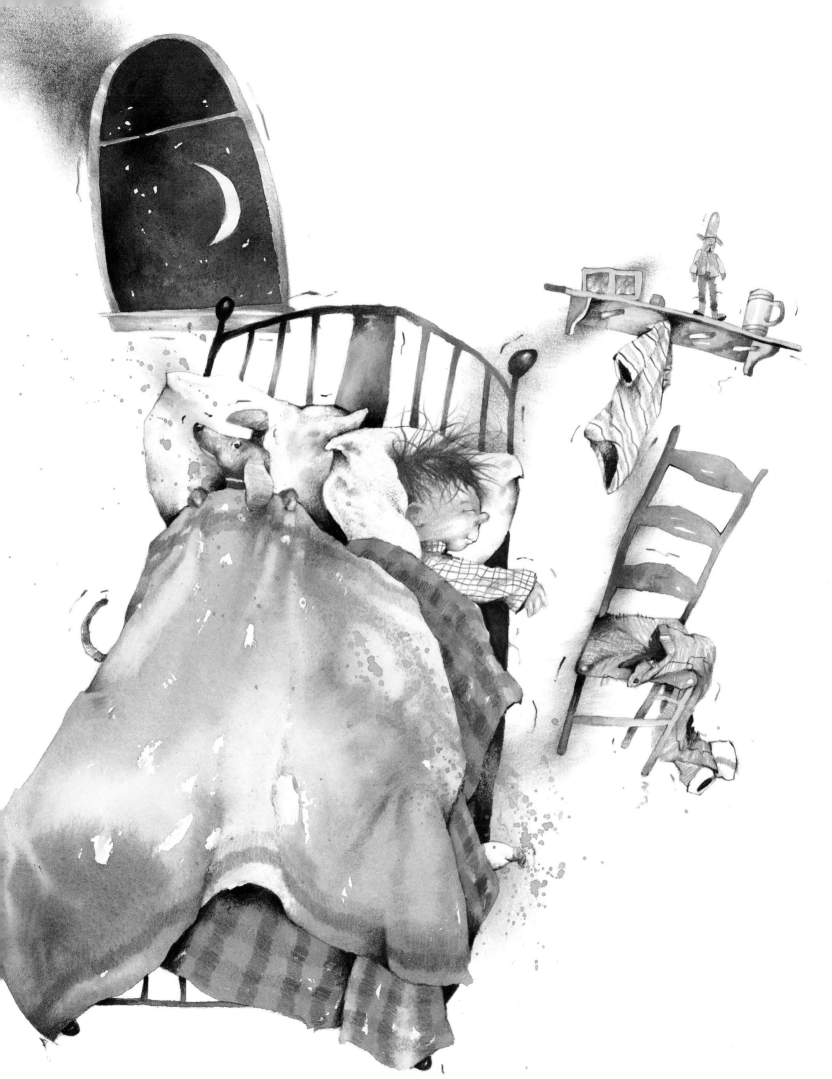

A sheriff arrived on a horse the next day.
He was careful to stay several houses away.
From his horse, which was mouthing the single word, "Phew!"
he shouted to Tim, "I have orders for you!
We have passed a new law. Here it is, written down:
No stinky socks may be worn in this town.
So Timothy, Timothy, Timothy Cox,
won't you consider, please, changing your socks?"
Then, holding his nose, he exclaimed, "Giddy-up!"
"And it's just fifteen days," Timmy said to his pup.

The gripes and complaints, in what seemed a barrage,
poured in till his parents said, "Tim, the garage—
though you are a wonderful son in all ways—
might well be the place you should stay a few days."

Inside the garage Timmy set up a camp
with a cooler, a cot, his books, and a lamp.
He was eating a peach when he heard someone yell,
"Let's try to play, Tim, despite the bad smell!"

Outside were his neighbors, Art, June, and Pierre.
Art was holding his nose. June was fanning the air.
And Pierre—poor Pierre—he had practically fainted.
"The air," he was gasping, "the air, Tim, it's tainted!"

A panicky rabbit ran right past a cop,
who turned on his siren and forced him to stop,
and was telling him sternly, "Your speed is unlawful,"
when the rabbit said, "Sir, don't you smell something awful?"

The officer lifted his nose for a sniff.
He gagged and he choked at his very first whiff.
He phoned in the news to the guys at the station.
They sent out the 'copters with this declaration:
"Timothy, Timothy, Timothy Cox,
won't you consider, please, changing your socks?"
The 'copter propellers went *whup-whup-whup-whup*!
"Day twenty already," said Tim to his pup.

Next morning the fire department with hoses
came riding their engines and holding their noses.
They hopped down at once, and they started to spray.
Poor Timmy and Walt had to scamper away
down a path, into woods, up a hill, over rocks,
wilting flowers and plants with the stench of Tim's socks.
Tim circled around with the trucks in pursuit
and hurried back home by a quite different route.

At his house Timmy found a brief note on the gate.
"Your mother and I," wrote his dad, "hesitate
to find any fault with the way that you smell,
but, Timmy, we think it would be just as well
if you moved all your stuff to that comfortable spot
next to the fence at the end of our lot."
He had signed it, "Your father, your best, truest friend.
P.S. The *farthest,* the most *extreme* end!"
In a scrawl his dad added, "P.P.S. My son,
your homework's a thing we *assume* you'll get done!"

Walter helped Timothy move out his stuff,
saying wearily, "Timmy, enough is enough.
Haven't you proved what you wanted to prove?
How far from the house must your folks make you move?"

"Faithful dog," Timmy said, "as you know, I'm the kind
who follows things through once he's made up his mind.
I will not be discouraged. I won't be deterred.
And that, my dear Walter, is my final word."

Walter was helping Tim carry his cot,
and it *can't* be repeated—the things that dog thought!

Tim, with his hat and his food and his dog,
found the spot by the fence. It was nearly a bog.
There were various grasses in various clumps,
mosquitoes and blue flies and green flies and stumps,
and a skunk who was grinning as hard as he could.
"Gosh," he told Timmy, "you smell really good!"

All through the night there was racket, of course,
from loudspeaker trucks that had come out in force
to drive every road, every lane, every street
with a warning to Timmy concerning his feet.
"Timothy, Timothy, Timothy Cox,
won't you consider, please, changing your socks?
You've been yelled at and chased, and you ought to give up!"
"Only three days to go!" Tim exclaimed to his pup.

The next day came and went, with the temperature freezing.
Walt shivered. Tim shook. And the skunk started sneezing.
They tried to keep warm with some running and stretching.
What gripes from the neighborhood, though. What kvetching!
People were gagging. They shouted, "We're sick!
You must change those socks, and you must do it quick!"
"Pay no attention," Tim said to his friends.
"There's two days remaining before this thing ends."

Scouts, the next day from the fringes of trees,
spelled out with their flags, "Timmy, change your socks, *please!*"
Judges banged gavels, and referees whistled.
The governor glowered. His honor guard bristled.

Even the skunk, their new friend, had to quit.
"Your smell," he told Timmy, "I have to admit—
though by nature I'm one who's reluctant to nag—
at moments has made even *me* want to gag!"
He shook hands with Walter and Timmy, and then
as the sun slowly set, he went home to his den.

The sinking sun tinted the sky's arching vault
as Tim shared his thoughts with his faithful dog, Walt.
"Almost a month has gone by to the day,
and do I regret what I've done, Walt? No way!
I'd do it again. And I know you would too."
Walter replied very coolly, "*Not* true."

The month! The whole month! It ended at dawn!
Tim pulled off the stockings that he'd first put on
a full month before, a full month to the day,
and Walter, who watched him, said weakly, "Hooray.
Timothy, Timothy, Timothy Cox,
at last you have changed those abominable socks.
You've followed things through, as you said way back then,
but please, Timmy, *don't ever do it again!*"

In a case full of trophies, which no one unlocks,
the school still displays Timmy's raggedy socks
with a sign that declares Timmy followed things through,
and others might think about doing that too.

Timmy himself, if you go look him up,
will tell you the same, till a nudge from his pup
reminds him to say what he now knows is true:
"Though it's right and it's good that you follow things through,
resist the temptation to waste your ambition
on some sort of silly or trivial mission.
The wise thing to do is to think and to plan—
which I *didn't* do. But I'm sure that *you* can!"

With love to my son, Chevy, and my daughter, Alice—R. K.

To Sharon, who always smells nice—S. G.

SIMON & SCHUSTER BOOKS FOR YOUNG READERS
An imprint of Simon & Schuster Children's Publishing Division
1230 Avenue of the Americas, New York, New York 10020
Text copyright © 2005 by Robert Kinerk
Illustrations copyright © 2005 by Stephen Gammell
SIMON & SCHUSTER BOOKS FOR YOUNG READERS is a trademark of Simon & Schuster, Inc.
Book design by Mark Siegel
The text for this book is set in GoudySans.
The illustrations for this book are rendered in watercolor, colored pencil, and pastel.
Manufactured in China
10 9 8 7 6 5 4 3 2 1
Library of Congress Cataloging-in-Publication Data
Kinerk, Robert.
Timothy Cox will not change his socks / Robert Kinerk ; illustrated by Stephen Gammell.—1st ed.
p. cm.
"A Paula Wiseman book."
Summary: Timothy Cox, who is good at following through on ideas, decides to wear the same unwashed socks for one month, ignoring the objections of his dachsund, Walt, and everyone else around him.
ISBN 0-689-87181-3
[1. Odors—Fiction. 2. Socks—Fiction. 3. Perseverance (Ethics)—Fiction. 4. Dachshunds—Fiction. 5. Dogs—Fiction.
6. Stories in rhyme.] I. Gammell, Stephen, ill. II. Title.
PZ8.3.K566 Ti 2005
[E]—dc22
2003025412